D0580039

CALGARY PUBLIC LIBRARY

OCT   2015

My SELF Bookshelf

The Three Pig Sisters

By Cecil Kim

Illustrated by Keun Park

Language Arts Consultant: Joy Cowley

NORWOOD HOUSE PRESS

Chicago, Illinois

DEAR CAREGIVER — My**SELF** Bookshelf is a series of books that support children's social emotional learning. SEL has been proven to promote not only the development of self-awareness, responsibility, and positive relationships, but also academic achievement.

Current research reveals that the part of the brain that manages emotion is directly connected to the part of the brain that is used in cognitive tasks, such as: problem solving, logic, reasoning, and critical thinking—all of which are at the heart of learning.

SEL is also directly linked to what are referred to as 21st Century Skills: collaboration, communication, creativity, and critical thinking. MySELF Bookshelf offers an early start that will help children build the competencies for success in school and life.

In these delightful books, young children practice early reading skills while learning how to manage their own feelings and how to be considerate of other perspectives. Each book focuses on aspects of SEL that help children develop social competence that will benefit them in their relationships with others as well as in their school success. The charming characters in the stories model positive traits such as: responsibility, goal setting, determination, patience, and celebrating differences. At the end of each story, you will find a letter that highlights the positive traits and an activity or discussion to help your child apply SEL to his or her own life.

Above all, the most important part of the reading experience is to have fun and enjoy it!

Sincerely,

Shannon Cannon

Shannon Cannon, Ph.D.
Literacy and SEL Consultant

Norwood House Press • P.O. Box 316598 • Chicago, Illinois 60631
For more information about Norwood House Press please visit our website at www.norwoodhousepress.com or call 866-565-2900.

Shannon Cannon – Literacy and SEL Consultant
Joy Cowley – English Language Arts Consultant
Mary Lindeen – Consulting Editor

© Norwood House Press 2015. All Rights Reserved. No part of this book may be reproduced or utilized in any form or by any means without written permission from the publisher. Original Korean Text © Cecil Kim 2011. Illustrations Copyright © Keun Park 2011. Original Korean Edition © Eenbook Co. 2011. This English Edition published under license from Big & Small Publishing.

Library of Congress Cataloging-in-Publication Data
    Kim, Cecil.
    The three pig sisters / by Cecil Kim ; illustrated by Keun Park.
        pages cm. -- (MySelf bookshelf)
    Summary: "The three pig sisters begin building their home, cautiously avoiding the wolf. When two sisters eat sleeping berries and fall victim to the wolf, the sisters work together to teach the wolf a lesson. Realizing the wolf is just old and hungry, the sisters and wolf work to make a farm and together grow fruits and vegetables"-- Provided by publisher.
    ISBN 978-1-59953-654-5 (library edition : alk. paper) -- ISBN 978-1-60357-714-4 (ebook)
    [1. Cooperativeness--Fiction. 2. Pigs--Fiction. 3. Sisters--Fiction. 4. Wolves--Fiction. 5. House construction--Fiction.] I. Park, Keun, illustrator. II. Title.
    PZ7.K55958Th 2015
    [E]--dc23

                                        2014030345

Manufactured in the United States of America in Stevens Point, Wisconsin.
263N—122014

The three pig sisters were ready to leave home.
They would make a new house in the woods.
Their mother worried about them.
"My dears, have you heard the story
of the three pigs and the big bad wolf?
Make sure you build solid houses
to keep you safe from wolves."

4

5

The sisters thought about their mother's words.
The oldest sister said, "Those pigs made a mistake.
They built three different houses."

The middle sister said, "If we work together,
we can make one very strong house for all of us."

"You are so right," said the youngest sister.

The next morning, the three sisters left home.
Tears streamed from their mother's eyes,
and she mopped her face with her apron.
"Do be careful, dear children," she said.

"Don't worry, Mother," they said.
"We will build a very strong house,
and we will defeat any wolf
that comes our way."

When the sisters arrived in the woods,
they found a place to build their house.
They divided the work three ways.
"I will clear the ground for our home,"
said the oldest sister.
"I will get logs from the woods,"
said the middle sister.
"I will make the bricks,"
said the youngest sister.

While the oldest pig cleared the ground,
the middle pig went to get logs.
On the way, she saw some tasty berries.
She decided to eat a few.

In order to make the bricks,
the youngest pig needed water.
Near the stream she found some berries.
She decided to eat a few.

The two sisters did not know that the berries
were sleeping berries. Soon the two pigs
were fast asleep.
The wolf, who had been watching,
rubbed his paws together. "Ha ha!
It has been a long time since I last ate.
Those two pigs look delicious!"

At that moment, the oldest pig called,
"Sisters! Sisters! Where are you?"

The wolf left the sleeping pigs
and ran away to hide.

The oldest pig woke her sisters.
"Why aren't you working?"

"We ate some red berries," they said.
"We fell asleep."

The oldest pig sniffed the berries.
Then she saw the wolf's footprints.
"A wolf!" she cried. "Hurry, Sisters!
We must work together
and build our strong house."

The three sisters worked hard,
cutting down trees and making bricks.

18

They set up strong wooden pillars.
They built strong brick walls.
They made doors and windows
and a shiny red roof.
They had a beautiful strong house.

19

But the three pig sisters
had one more job to do.
They had to take care
of the big bad wolf.
So they made a pot of soup
and opened the windows.

The hungry wolf sniffed the air.
A delicious smell came from the pigs' house,
but the house was too strong to blow down.
The wolf had to find another way.

He remembered the trouble he'd had
getting down the chimney of another pig's house.
He would have to break this door down.

24

The wolf ran at the door, but it was open and he fell right into the house. Crash! "Why was it so dark?" he wondered.

Then he heard voices.
"I'll tie his front legs together."
"I'll tie his back legs together."
"I'll feed him sleeping berries."

When the wolf woke up,
he was tied tightly to a chair.

"Shall we drop him down a well?"
asked the oldest pig sister.

"No, no!" cried the wolf. "Please don't.
I only bothered you because I'm hungry.
An old wolf like me can't hunt for food."

What would the pig sisters do?

They decided to work with the wolf
to make a farm on their land.
The oldest pig grew corn.
The middle pig grew potatoes.
The youngest pig grew apple trees
with sweet juicy apples.

28

What did the wolf do?
He weeded the gardens
and looked after the chickens.

29

Food filled the table in the strong house.
"It is great to work together!"
said the wolf to the three pig sisters.
What he said was indeed true,
and they all lived and worked together
happily for a long, long time.

Dear Wolf,

We are so happy you decided to come live with us and work with us. As sisters, we are used to working together on things. We could build a strong house because we worked together on it. With each of us doing part of the job, we finished our house in no time. We were even able to trick you and catch you by working together!

Now that you are working with us too, we can all enjoy the delicious food that comes from our beautiful farm. We think that is the best way for all of us to find something good to eat!

Thank you for working together with us.

Your friends, The Three Pig Sisters

SOCIAL AND EMOTIONAL LEARNING FOCUS

Working as a Team

Both the wolf and the three pig sisters tried to trick each other. In the end they decided to work together. This made them all happier and they got more done.

Teamwork and collaboration are very important skills for success in life. If you have ever played on a team, you know that everyone must do their part and work together toward a common goal. Collaboration means to work with another person or group to accomplish something.

Team building can be a lot of fun. Here's one way to learn to collaborate and build trust.

Human Knot

This is a problem-solving activity that needs at least four people.

- Get in a tight circle facing each other. Your shoulders should be touching.
- Reach in to the circle and grasp the hands of two different people.
- Take a small step back to see how everyone is tangled.
- Untangle the knot without letting go of hands.
- Use encouraging words to help each other untie the human knot.

Reader's Theater

Reader's Theater is an interactive approach to reading that allows students to understand each story through dramatic interpretation. By involving students in reading, listening, and speaking activities, they provide an integrated approach for students to develop fluency and comprehension. A Reader's Theater edition of this book is available online. You can access the script by scanning the QR code to the right or visit our website at: http://www.norwoodhousepress.com/threepigsisters.aspx